Substitute
TEACHER PLANS

DOUG JOHNSON

illustrated by

TAMMY SMITH

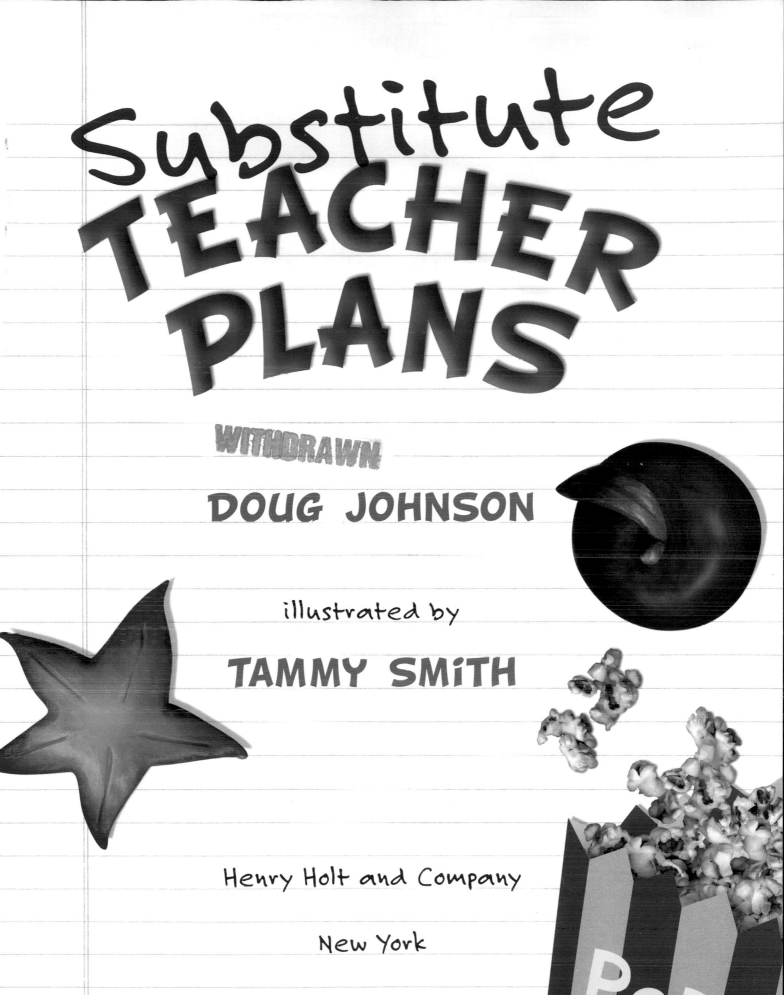

Henry Holt and Company

New York

Henry Holt and Company, LLC

Publishers since 1866

175 Fifth Avenue

New York, New York 10010

www.henryholtchildrensbooks.com

Distributed in Canada by H. B. Fenn and Company Ltd.

Library of Congress Cataloging-in-Publication Data

Johnson, Doug. Substitute teacher plans / by Doug Johnson; illustrated by Tammy Smith.

Summary: Miss Huff prepares an unusual list of activities for the substitute teacher

who is covering her class when she takes a much needed day off.

[1. Substitute teachers—Fiction. 2. Teachers—Fiction. 3.Schools-Fiction.

4. Humorous stories.] I. Smith, Tammy, ill. II. Title.

PZ7.J631715 Su 2002   [E]—dc21   2001003720

ISBN-10: 0-8050-6520-2 / ISBN-13: 978-0-8050-6520-6

First Edition-2002 / Designed by Donna Mark

Manufactured in China

3 5 7 9 10 8 6 4

The artist used clay, acrylic, collage, and the computer program
Photoshop® to create the illustrations for this book.

To God who loves me, and
to all the teachers and their substitute teachers
who care so much for their students
— D. J.

To Mike and Murphy
— T. S.

Miss Huff looked over her class and sighed deeply.

Sarah was sticking out her tongue at Billy.

Billy was making faces at Carl.

Nancy blew such a big bubble that she floated across the room and got stuck in Francine's hair.

Allen was swinging on a rope hooked to the lights, pretending that he was Tarzan screaming, "AAAAA-EEEEEE-AAHHHHHH!"

Greg was growling like a wild animal.

"I need a break," Miss Huff moaned. "I need a vacation day!"

That night she decided to make up a list of substitute teacher plans and a list of fun things that she could do on her day off.

Miss Huff did her substitute teacher plans first. Then she began her list of fun things to do. She got VERY excited and happily wrote and giggled through the night.

The next morning a very tired Miss Huff glanced at her two lists. "Oops," she thought, "I forgot to write Substitute Teacher Plans on the top of this list."

Poor Miss Huff was so exhausted, though, that she wrote it down on her OWN list of fun things to do. Then Miss Huff drove to school and put the wrong list on her desk for the substitute teacher.

A little while later Miss Huff rushed back home and looked over her list of things to do on her day off. The first activity said:

READING — 9:15 TO 10:30.

"Oh, goody," she chuckled, "I just love to read!" Miss Huff plopped down in a chair with a joke book. Before long she was giggling and laughing and rolling on the floor. Even her cat, Rudy, joined in.

Back at school Mrs. Martin the substitute teacher looked at her list of plans. The first activity said:

RIDE THE ROLLER COASTER AT OCEAN PARK.

"Hmmm," said Mrs. Martin, "I'll need a bus to get us there." She called the front office for assistance. Before long she and the children were buzzing on the gigantic roller coaster with their hands in the air. "Whee!" they screamed. "Yahoo," laughed Mrs. Martin in return.

At home sweet home Miss Huff set her joke book down and read the next activity on her list. It said:

WRITING — 10:30 TO 11:00.

"Ahh," sighed Miss Huff. "Just what I've been wanting to do." She brought out her address book and began writing to all her relatives and friends. It felt good to stay in touch. She smiled as she wrote.

Back at school Mrs. Martin looked at her list of plans. The next activity said:

SKYDIVING.

Mrs. Martin made sure all the children's parachutes were fastened tightly as the plane sliced through the air.

"Okay, kids, on the count of three, we zip out the door one by one as quickly as we can. ONE . . . TWO . . . THREE! GERONIMO!" The children formed a gigantic star. It was a sight to see.

At home sweet home Miss Huff looked at her list. It said:

SPELLING — 11:00 TO 11:30.

She and Rudy played Scrabble. Miss Huff won. Rudy growled.

Back at school Mrs. Martin gazed at her list of plans.
The next activity said:

SCUBA DIVING.

It was very exciting for the children to swim in the water
with all the marine life. They watched in amazement as the
octopus playfully pulled Mrs. Martin through the water.

At home sweet home Miss Huff gazed at her list. The next activity said:

LUNCH AND RECESS — 11:30 TO 12:30.

After eating a peanut butter and jelly sandwich, Miss Huff played hopscotch with Rudy. Rudy won. Miss Huff growled.

Back at school Mrs. Martin looked at her list of plans.
The next activity said:

LUNCH ON MOUNTAINTOP AND SKI DOWN.

The bus strained as it climbed the tallest mountain
imaginable. It was called Forever Snow Mountain.

After lunch the children zigged and zagged down the slope, while Mrs. Martin accidentally set a record for the longest ski jump. All the children clapped when she landed on one ski.

At home sweet home Miss Huff looked at her list. The next activity said:

READ BOOK ALOUD — 12:30 TO 1:00.

Miss Huff read to Rudy. Rudy purred.

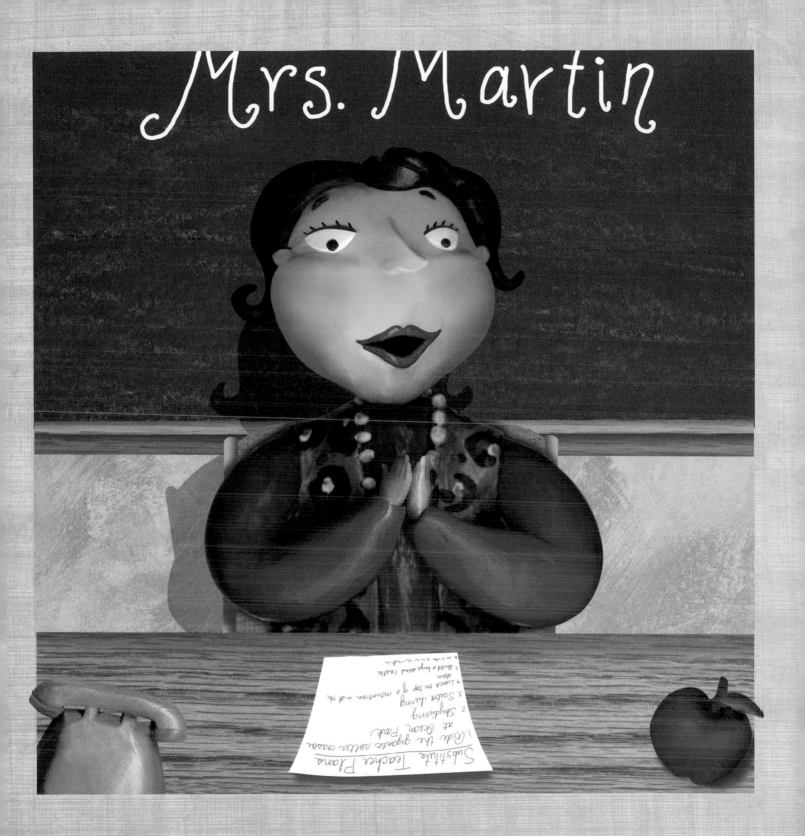

Back at school Mrs. Martin looked at her list of plans. It said:

BUILD HUGE SAND CASTLE.

When they got to the beach Mrs. Martin rented a steam shovel.
She and the children created an amazing castle. It was HUGE!
It even had a helicopter landing pad.

At home sweet home Miss Huff whispered to herself, "I sure feel rested." She looked at her list. The next activity said:

MATH — 1:00 TO 2:00.

"Hmmm, I've always loved math." She pulled out her checkbook and paid her bills. She felt wonderful.

Back at school Mrs. Martin looked at her list
of plans and smiled.

In no time at all, the children were at the circus. They laughed at the clowns, clapped for the trapeze artists, and gasped at the lion tamer, who just happened to be Mrs. Martin. That's why Mrs. Martin was such a great substitute teacher. Anybody who could train lions could handle kids.

At the end of the day, after Mrs. Martin excused the children, she wrote a note to their teacher.

Miss Huff

Dear Miss Huff,
I had a terrific day. You
write very good substitute
teacher plans. The children
were well behaved—much
better than the lions!
Sincerely,
Mrs. Martin

The next day at school Miss Huff felt very energetic. She was teaching up a storm—until the principal walked in with the list of yesterday's activities.

"Miss Huff, I think you have some explaining to do," he said and handed her the list.

"Goodness sakes," said Miss Huff. "I need another vacation day!"

Now, although the children had fun with Mrs. Martin, they really loved Miss Huff, even if they didn't always show it. "Oh, please, Miss Huff," they chorused. "Please be here tomorrow!"

Miss Huff looked at her students, then glanced at the list again and shook her head. She reached for the phone.

"I would like to make a reservation for acrobatic flight training tomorrow," she said.

All the children sighed.

"For how many?" Miss Huff winked. "Well, one adult and . . . TWENTY-FIVE CHILDREN! And we might as well bring along our principal!"